D1238977

Book Club Edition

WALT DISNEY PRODUCTIONS

presents

Scamp and the Kitten

Random House New York

 Published in the United States by Random House, Inc., New York, and simultaneously in Canada by Random House of Canada Limited, Toronto. Originally published in Denmark as VAKS OG KILLINGEN ROSE by Gutenberghus Gruppen, Copenhagen. ISBN: 0-394-86319-4 Manufactured in the United States of America

3 4 5 6 7 8 9 0 A B C D E F G H I J K

One day Aunt Sara came
to visit Eric and his mother, Darling.
She brought her little kitten,
Pumpkin, with her.

"It's a beautiful day," said Darling. "Let's go to the park."

"Woof, woof!" said the four puppies who lived with Darling and Eric.

And so they all went off to the park.
Scamp the puppy led the way.
Aunt Sara held on tight to her kitten.

Aunt Sara and Darling sat down on a park bench to talk.

Eric and the four puppies ran off to play ball.

The sun was hot.

By and by Aunt Sara and Darling fell asleep.

Pumpkin the kitten jumped out of Aunt Sara's lap.

Pumpkin ran happily off.
She saw the puppies with Eric.

"I want to play too!"
said Pumpkin.

But when Pumpkin came closer, she decided not to play after all.

The ball game was too rough and noisy for her.

Scamp saw the kitten.

"Hello, there," he said. "Come play with us!"

"No, thank you," said Pumpkin. "I have a much better game. It's called Butterfly. Bye-bye."

And the kitten chased after a butterfly.
"Wait!" called Scamp.
He went after the kitten.

Pumpkin ran out of the park.
Scamp followed her.

Scamp did not want Pumpkin to get lost.
She had been lost once before.
Scamp had found her for Aunt Sara.

Pumpkin jumped into a box.

Scamp jumped up after her.

"Scamp is playing chase with me," thought Pumpkin. "What fun!"

And she jumped down and ran off.

"Stop! Come back!" called Scamp.

The kitten ran into the street.
She didn't see the big truck.
And the truckdriver didn't see her!

Scamp had to do something fast.

He ran into the street right in front of the truck.

SCREECH! The truck stopped.

"What a brave puppy!" said the driver.

Scamp jumped back onto the sidewalk.
But the kitten ran the other way.
"Oh, no!" said Scamp.

Pumpkin was scared by all the noisy cars and trucks. She ran away—fast!

Now Scamp was all alone.

"Where, oh where, is that kitten?" he wondered.

He looked here...

and there...

and everywhere.

No kitten!

Pumpkin wandered all day.
It stopped being fun.

She couldn't find Scamp.
She couldn't find Aunt Sara
Pumpkin was really lost!

Suddenly Pumpkin heard a growl.
She saw dogs.
BIG MEAN DOGS!
“Meow! Meow!” yelled the kitten.

And she started to run.

Pumpkin ran as fast as her little legs could go.

The big dogs ran after her.

"Arf, arf! Bow-wow! GRRRRRR!" went the dogs.

Poor Pumpkin was so scared!

Suddenly Scamp heard a kitten's "Meow!"
"That's Pumpkin!" he said.

And off he went.

"ME-OWWW!"

Scamp heard the kitten cry again.

The puppy followed the sound.

He took a big jump and landed on a wall.

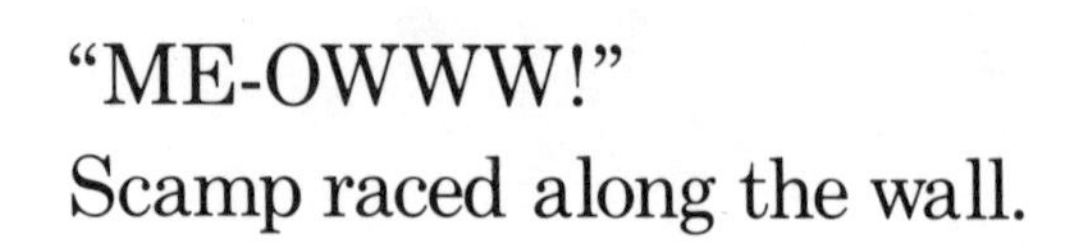

"ME-OWWW!"
Scamp raced along the wall.

Scamp saw the big dogs.
They had cornered Pumpkin.
"Stop!" yelled Scamp.

Scamp jumped right in front of the big dogs.

The dogs barked at Scamp.

But Scamp barked right back at them.

He was very angry at them for scaring Pumpkin.

A policeman heard the noise.

He came running up.

"What's going on here?" he shouted.

The big dogs quickly ran away.
The policeman picked up Pumpkin.
"Nice kitty," he said. "And you are a brave little puppy!" he said to Scamp.
"Woof!" said Scamp.

The policeman looked at Scamp's dog tag.
He saw Scamp's name and address.

"Time to go home," said the policeman.

“Lead the way, Scamp,” said the policeman. “You are a good dog!”

"Woof!" said Scamp.

He barked and jumped and ran all the way home.

But the kitten went to sleep in the policeman's arms.

At home everyone was worried.

"Where can they be?" said Darling to her husband, Jim.

"Don't worry," said Jim. "I know Scamp will look after Pumpkin. Remember how he found Pumpkin the last time she was lost?"

Just then the doorbell rang.

“Good evening,” said the policeman at the door. “Do you know this kitten and puppy?”

And he told how Scamp had saved Pumpkin from the big dogs.

Scamp and Pumpkin got big hugs.
"Good dog, Scamp!" said Darling and Jim.
Scamp's parents, Lady and the Tramp, smiled proudly at their son.

Then all the people went upstairs to bed.

And all the pets settled down for the night.
Pumpkin curled up next to Scamp.
"Purr-r-r," she went.
"Sweet dreams," growled Scamp.